A NOTE TO PARENTS

Reading Aloud with Your Child

Research shows that reading books aloud is the single most valuable support parents can provide in helping children learn to read.

- Be a ham! The more enthusiasm you display, the more your child will enjoy the book.
- Run your finger underneath the words as you read to signal that the print carries the story.
- Leave time for examining the illustrations more closely; encourage your child to find things in the pictures.
- Invite your youngster to join in whenever there's a repeated phrase in the text.
- Link up events in the book with similar events in your child's life.
- If your child asks a question, stop and answer it. The book can be a means to learning more about your child's thoughts.

Listening to Your Child Read Aloud

The support of your attention and praise is absolutely crucial to your child's continuing efforts to learn to read.

- If your child is learning to read and asks for a word, give it immediately so that the meaning of the story is not interrupted. DO NOT ask your child to sound out the word.
- On the other hand, if your child initiates the act of sounding out, don't intervene.
- If your child is reading along and makes what is called a miscue, listen for the sense of the miscue. If the word "road" is substituted for the word "street," for instance, no meaning is lost. Don't stop the reading for a correction.
- If the miscue makes no sense (for example, "horse" for "house"), ask your child to reread the sentence because you're not sure you understand what's just been read.
- Above all else, enjoy your child's growing command of print and make sure you give lots of praise. *You are your child's first teacher—and the most important one. Praise from you is critical for further risk-taking and learning.*

—Priscilla Lynch
Ph.D., New York University
Educational Consultant

Roller

Text copyright © 1992 by Stephanie Calmenson.
Illustrations copyright © 1992 by True Kelley.
All rights reserved. Published by Scholastic Inc.
HELLO READER!, CARTWHEEL BOOKS, and the CARTWHEEL BOOKS logo
are registered trademarks of Scholastic Inc.

ISBN 0-590-50940-3

12 11 10 9 8 7 6 5 4 3   8   7 8 9/9 0/0

Printed in the U.S.A.

37

Skates!

By Stephanie Calmenson
Illustrated by True Kelley

Hello Reader! — Level 2

SCHOLASTIC INC.
New York Toronto London Auckland Sydney

Early one morning
in a small sleepy town,
six trucks rumbled up
and boxes came down.

Sam Skipper called out
as the trucks drove away,
"Two boxes were all
that I needed today!"

He counted the boxes.
There were fifty-two.
He sat down and said,
"Now what will I do?"

Soon an idea
popped into Sam's head.
He made up a sign
and here's what it said:
BIG SALE TODAY ON
ROLLER SKATES!

BIG SALE
TODAY
ON
ROLLER SKATES!
SKATES
SKATES
SKATES
SKATES
SKATES
SKATES
SKATES
SKATES

People came
from far and wide.
There were even people
who never had tried
to get around on
roller skates.

The Bensons were out
for their afternoon stroll.
Then they decided
to go out and roll!
The Bensons got four pairs of
roller skates.

Joe, the mail carrier, said,
"Skates will be great!
I can go fast,
and the mail won't be late!"
He delivered the mail on
roller skates.

Anna Lee
knew what to do.
She strapped on one.
She strapped on two.
She jumped and twirled on her
roller skates.

Pizza stays hot
when you soar down the street.
For delivering pizza,
skates can't be beat!
Watch out for Pete on his
roller skates.

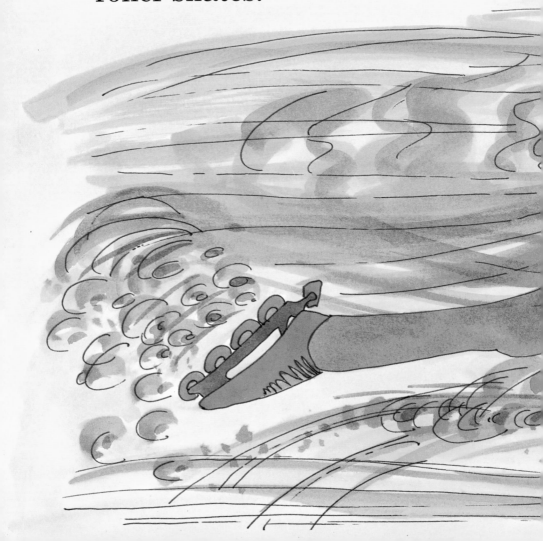

Shopping for supper
is no longer a chore.
Martha fills up her basket
as she zips through the store.
It's fun to shop on
roller skates.

Sam, Sue, and Sal like
how it feels when
Mommy and Daddy
take them out on wheels.
Someday they will *all* go on
roller skates!

Be careful, Billy.
Don't go too fast.
Your ice-cream cone
will never last.
It's hard to eat ice cream on
roller skates.

Jordan's daddy
drove to work in his car,
even though his office
was not very far.
Now Daddy is cool on his
roller skates.

Jill's job walking dogs
became a breeze.
She rolled along
the street with ease.
The dogs pull Jill on her
roller skates.

Now in this lively town,
all the people agree
that life is as easy
as it can be...

when everyone rides on
roller skates!